W9-AYA-862

Squire Trelawney and Dr. Livesey having asked me to write down the whole particulars about Treasure Island, from the beginning to the end, I take up my pen, and go back to the time when my father kept the "Admiral Benbow" inn.

I remember, as if it were yesterday, the brown old seaman with the sabre cut across one cheek...as he came plodding along the cove.

I remember him breaking out in that old sea-song he sang so often afterwards:

"FIFTEEN MEN ON THE DEAD MAN'S CHEST— YO-HO-HO, AND A BOTTLE OF RUM!..."♪

Spotlight

MARVEL®

Treasure Island

Adapted from the novel by Robert Louis Stevenson

Vol. 1: Treasure Island

Roy Thomas *writer*   Mario Gully *penciler*   Pat Davidson *inker*   SotoColor's A. Crossley *colorist*   VC's Joe Caramagna *letterer*   Nicole Boose *associate editor*   Ralph Macchio *editor*   Joe Quesada *editor in chief*   Dan Buckley *publisher*

His sea-chest following behind him in a handbarrow, he trudged heavily...

...right up to the inn door.

RAP RAP RAP

When my father appeared, he called out roughly...

I be wantin' a bottle o' rum!

This is a handy cove...

Y-Yes... here you are, my good man.

...and a pleasant situated grog-shop.

Much company, matey?

No, very little, the more's the pity.

Well, then, this is the berth for me.

You can call me "Captain"!

Tell him to pipe all hands--magistrates and such--and he'll soon find all old Flint's crew, man and boy, at the *"Admiral Benbow"*!

I was old Cap'n Flint's first mate, Jim-- and I'm the only one as knows the place!

He gave it to me when he lay a-dyin'.

They're after my sea-chest-- Black Dog, and that seafarin' man with one leg...him above all...!

What's the *"black spot"*?

That's a summons, mate.

But you keep your weather-eye open--and I'll share with you equal--

--upon my honor...

He wandered a little longer, his voice growing weaker.

After I had given him his medicine, he fell into a heavy, swoon-like sleep.

Probably I should have told the whole story to the doctor...

But, as things fell out, my poor father died suddenly that evening...

...which put all other matters on one side.

Next morning, though weak, the captain got downstairs and had more food... and rum...

...his cutlass lying bare before him on the table.

Filled with hope, we hurried upstairs to the little room where he had slept so long...

...and where his box had stood since the day of his arrival.

A strong smell of tobacco and tar rose from the interior...

Echh...

Give me the key.

Beneath a suit of good clothes on top, the miscellany began...

Nothing of any value save that pistol...and a piece of bar silver...

But what's this?

A bundle tied up in oilcloth...

...and a canvas bag... that jingles!

Coins...of all countries and sizes... all shaken together at random.

I'll show these rogues that I'm an honest woman.

I'll have my dues, and not a farthing ov--

Mother... listen!

It's him!

TAP TAP TAP

VISIT US AT
www.abdopublishing.com

Reinforced library bound edition published in 2009 by Spotlight, a division of the ABDO Group, 8000 West 78th Street, Edina, Minnesota 55439. Spotlight produces high-quality reinforced library bound editions for schools and libraries. Published by agreement with Marvel Characters, Inc.

Copyright © 2009 Marvel Entertainment, Inc. and its subsidiaries. MARVEL, all related characters and the distinctive likenesses thereof: TM & © 2009 Marvel Entertainment, Inc. and its subsidiaries. Licensed by Marvel Characters B.V. www.marvel.com. All rights reserved.

Library of Congress Cataloging-in-Publication Data

Thomas, Roy, 1940-
  Treasure Island / adapted from the novel by Robert Louis Stevenson ; Roy Thomas, writer ; Mario Gully, penciler ; Pat Davidson, inker ; SotoColor's A. Crossley, colorist ; VC's Joe Caramagna, letterer. -- Reinforced library bound ed.
      v. cm.
   "Marvel."
   Contents: v. 1. Treasure Island -- v. 2. Treasure Island part 2 -- v. 3. Mutiny on the Hispaniola -- v. 4. Embassy--and attack -- v. 5. In the enemy's camp -- v. 6. Pirates' end?
   ISBN 9781599616018 (v. 1) -- ISBN 9781599616025 (v. 2) -- ISBN 9781599616032 (v. 3) -- ISBN 9781599616049 (v. 4) -- ISBN 9781599616056 (v. 5) -- ISBN 9781599616063 (v. 6)
   Summary: Retells, in comic book format, Robert Louis Stevenson's tale of an innkeeper's son who finds a treasure map that leads him to a pirate's fortune.
   [1. Stevenson, Robert Louis, 1850-1894. --Adaptations. 2. Graphic novels. 3. Buried treasure--Fiction. 4.Pirates--Fiction. 5. Adventure and adventurers--Fiction. 6. Caribbean Area--History--18th century--Fiction.] I. Stevenson, Robert Louis, 1850-1894. II. Gully, Mario. III. Davidson, Pat, 1965- IV. Crossley, Andrew. V. Caramagna, Joe. VI. Title.
PZ7.7.T518 Tre 2009
[Fic]--dc22   2008035322

All Spotlight books have reinforced library bindings and are manufactured in the United States of America.